JOHN CENA
ELBOW GREASE
Cleanup Crew

Illustrated by Dave Aikins

A Random House PICTUREBACK® Book

Random House 🏠 New York

Copyright © 2022 by John F. A. Cena Entertainment, Inc.
All rights reserved. Published in the United States by Random House Children's Books, a division of
Penguin Random House LLC, New York. Pictureback, Random House, and the Random House colophon are
registered trademarks of Penguin Random House LLC.
Visit us on the Web! rhcbooks.com
Educators and librarians, for a variety of teaching tools, visit us at RHTeachersLibrarians.com
Library of Congress Cataloging-in-Publication Data is available upon request.
ISBN 978-0-593-37705-5 (trade) — ISBN 978-0-593-37706-2 (ebook)
Printed in the United States of America
10 9 8 7 6 5 4 3 2 1
First Edition
Random House Children's Books supports the First Amendment and celebrates the right to read.

It was Earth Day, and Elbow Grease planned to celebrate outdoors with his brothers and friends.

"How about we go to the beach?" suggested Mel.

"Great idea!" replied Elbow Grease.

"I'm excited about the beach," whispered Tank, "but what's Earth Day?"

"It's a day to show love for our planet," explained Pinball. "And it's a day to figure out how we can each help the environment in our own way."

Elbow Grease and his brothers zoomed off.
"Last one to the beach gets buried in the
sand!" said Flash before racing away.

But when the gang arrived at the beach, their fun screeched to a halt—there was trash everywhere!

"Litter is dangerous!" cried Elbow Grease. "It pollutes the water, which harms the plants and animals."

"Some people don't care about the environment," said Pinball with a sigh.

Mel was upset, too. But she had an idea!

"What this beach needs is a good cleaning," Mel said.
"Will you all help me?"

Elbow Grease lit up. "Of course! We can do it together!"

The monster trucks revved their engines and got to work.

The trucks rocketed down the beach, collecting litter as they went. They raced to see who could pick up the most.

Bye-bye, trash!

Farther down the shore, Mel found some other people who wanted to help. They were just as excited as the trucks were to clean the beach!

Mel put up signs encouraging people to recycle, with big arrows to help them find the correct containers.

"Great job, everyone!" said 'Bo. The monster trucks and Chopper were proud to do their part to help the planet.

Before long, the beach was litter-free. The animals and plants in the ocean were sure to be happy.

"Okay, team, you know what to do!" said Mel.

The gang was proud to clean up **the park**, but
the center of town needed a scrub-up, **too!**
"All we need is a little gumption . . . **and soon**
this place will be spotless!" said 'Bo.

As they were about to start a new round of cleaning up, Mel shouted, "Look! Everyone else is pitching in, too!"

The people who had cleaned up the beach
were now picking up trash around town.

Before long, the whole town was sparkling clean!

After all the hard work was done, the monster trucks decided to celebrate with an Earth Day parade!

Yay! I love parades!

Elbow Grease and his brothers led the way, but the true stars of the Earth Day parade were the town's new electric sanitation trucks! They would work hard each and every day to keep the community clean.

Hey! Those trucks are electric, just like me!

And me!

If everyone does their part, we can save our planet!